J Moss
Moss, Marissa
Alien Eraser to the rescue

This book belongs to:

I thought this
book was mine!

ALIEN ERASER IN THE INVASION BEGINS!

INVASIONS ARE COMPLICATED THINGS TO PLAN, BUT ALIEN ERASER IS PREPARED. HE HAS MAPS—MANY MAPS . . .

THE TRAFFIC ON EARTH IS WORSE THAN EVER. WHERE SHOULD I LAND? I DON'T WANT A PARKING TICKET!

. . . AND THE LATEST SCIENTIFIC METHODS.

EENY, MEENY, MINY, MOE!

HERE! THAT'S IT! ORDINARYVILLE, PLAINPLACE, USA!

HIS ARRIVAL GOES UNNOTICED.

I SEE A SHOOTING STAR.

OR AN ALIEN SPACESHIP ENTERING OUR ATMOSPHERE.

SAFELY LANDED, THE FIRST PART OF THE JOURNEY IS OVER. ALIEN ERASER WALKS FOR DAYS AND DAYS, SEARCHING FOR THE PERFECT TOOL FOR HIS SCHEMES.

I MUST FIND AN UNSUSPECTING HOST—SOMEONE WHO WILL THINK HE'S INVENTED ME AND WILL DRAW STORIES ABOUT ME. . . .

. . . SOMEONE I CAN USE TO RECOUNT MY GLORIOUS DEEDS.

ISN'T THERE ANYTHING TO EAT ON THIS FORSAKEN PLANET?

FINALLY:

THIS HOUSE LOOKS PROMISING. I'LL TRY HERE, AT LEAST TO FIND A SNACK.

WHO SLEEPS OBLIVIOUSLY IN HIS BED?

GNAAAK! SNORRT!

WHILE THE BOY SLUMBERS, ALIEN ERASER WORKS HIS MAGIC.

DREAM OF ME! DREAM OF ME! DREAM!

BUT HE MUST DO MORE THAN DREAM! HE MUST WRITE ABOUT ME. HOW ELSE WILL THIS WORLD KNOW OF MY GREAT EXPLOITS?

SEARCHING WILDLY THROUGH THE BOY'S BEDROOM, ALIEN ERASER LOOKS FOR SOMETHING, ANYTHING!

THIS ROOM IS A MESS!

UNTIL:

AHA!

THIS IS IT!

AN INNOCENT LOGBOOK OR . . .

THIS IS WHERE HE'LL WRITE ABOUT ME!

THE STORY OF ALIEN ERASER! TO READ MORE, TURN THE PAGE!

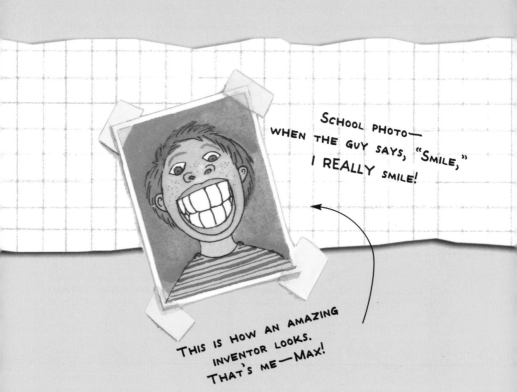

School photo—
when the guy says, "Smile,"
I REALLY smile!

This is how an amazing
inventor looks.
That's me—Max!

MAX DISASTER #1

Alien Eraser to the Rescue

Marissa Moss

CANDLEWICK PRESS

MYSTERIOUS MACHINE

BUNSEN BURNER

AH, THE SMELL OF FRESH-COOKED CHEMICALS!

BEAKERS OF STRANGE POWDERS AND FLUIDS

TONGS FOR PICKING GREEN THINGS OFF PIZZAS

BRIGHT IDEAS

MORE MYSTERIOUS MACHINES

STRANGE DIALS

POWERFUL
MAXBOT

PERCHLORICASAURUS

This is a book **I** found that's perfect for writing scientific stuff in.

There's a girl in my class who keeps a notebook about EVERYTHING in her life. SUPER BORING! I would never, I mean NEVER, do that, but suddenly, I have so many great ideas, I need a place to record them. I don't want to forget ANY of my cool inventions or experiments. My mom and dad are real scientists, and I'm going to be one, too.

SMELLY POTION

ROBOT TO PINCH PEOPLE'S NOSES IF THEY STICK THEM IN MY BUSINESS

Experiment #1
What happens when you microwave a marshmallow?

MAD SCIENTIST

HEE, HEE!
COME TO ME,
MY PRECIOUS SWEET
(OR SWEET PRECIOUS)!

O, INNOCENT
MARSHMALLOW,
WHOSE ONLY FEARS
INVOLVE CAMPFIRES
AND GRAHAM
CRACKERS, WHAT
STRANGE FATE
AWAITS YOU?

Steps

1. Put marshmallow on paper plate inside microwave oven.
2. Set for 40 to 60 seconds; hit Start button.
3. Stand back and watch the amazing transformation into . . .

Godzilla Puff!

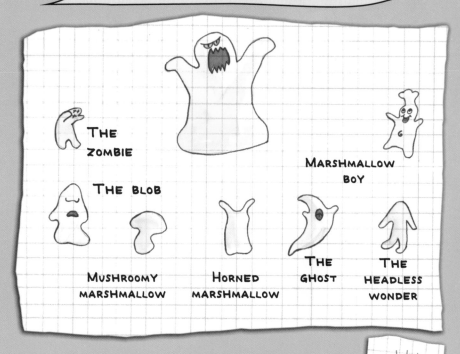

THE ZOMBIE

THE BLOB

MARSHMALLOW BOY

MUSHROOMY MARSHMALLOW

HORNED MARSHMALLOW

THE GHOST

THE HEADLESS WONDER

A WHOLE ARMY OF MUTANT MARSHMALLOWS

Observations: After 20 seconds, the marshmallow began to puff up. At 40 seconds, it was four times bigger than before.

Results: One angry mom for making a marshmallowy mess. But when I told Dad about it, he thought it was cool.

MAD MOTHER
(LOOKS KIND OF LIKE
A MAD SCIENTIST)

Dad tried to be the voice of reason.

That started another fight between Mom and Dad. It seems like they're always fighting these days. I still ended up being sent to my room, but that gave me the chance to work on one of my inventions.

Invention #1
A door alarm. If anyone comes into my room, a loud buzzer goes off.

BZZZZZZZZZZZZZZZZZZZ

Opening the door breaks the circuit, causing the alarm to sound.

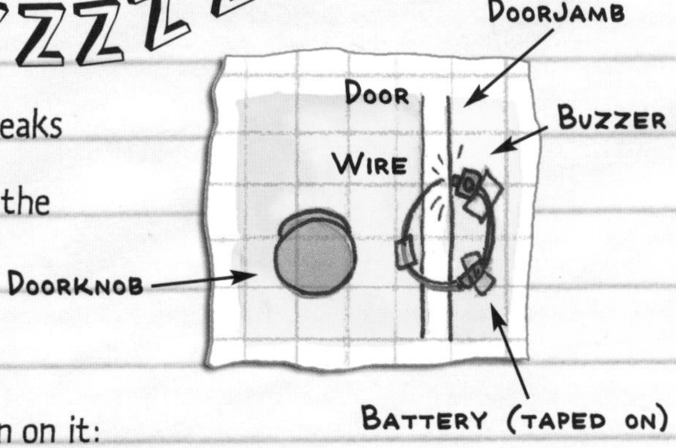

DOORJAMB
DOOR
BUZZER
WIRE
DOORKNOB
BATTERY (TAPED ON)

My door has this sign on it:

> WARNING! WARNING!
> All who enter must obey Max completely. NO TALKING, NO TOUCHING STUFF, and NO EATING LOUD APPLES!

APPLES ARE TOO CRUNCHY FOR MY DELICATE EARS (UNLESS I'M THE ONE EATING THEM).

That gave Kevin the idea to put this on HIS door:

> Only normal humans are allowed access to these quarters. Younger brothers are, by definition, neither normal nor human. By order of Kevin.

Too bad I can't invent a new family. If I could, I'd want to make a Robofamily, like this:

OLDER BROTHER WHO BURNS ANY CD I WANT.

MOM WHO GETS ME WHATEVER I ASK FOR. "HAVE SOME POPCORN AND SODA."

DAD WHO ALWAYS DOES STUFF WITH ME, LIKE SHOWING ME COOL THINGS AT HIS WORK AND TAKING ME OUT FOR PIZZA.

Instead, I made my perfect family out of that oh-so-useful school supply—the humble eraser:

ERASER DAD, HOLDING RUBBERY PIZZA.

ERASER ME, A BOUNCING, BALD BOY.

ERASER BROTHER—I CAN RUB HIM AWAY WHEN I GET MAD AT HIM.

ERASER MOM, HOLDING POPCORN.

I made a perfect teacher, too, the kind that lets me
do the science experiments I'm interested in, like:

(1) Testing the
chemical composition
of cafeteria food

 ERASER
SCIENCE
TEACHER

Smells
like
muddy
socks!

(2) Testing the bounciness
of leaky balls

FLOP

BLOP

PLOP

Bounce-O-Meter

VERY
BOUNCY!

IF YOU DON'T KICK IT,
YOU CAN MANAGE FINE.

DON'T EVEN
TRY!

But we don't have a perfect teacher. We have Ms. Blodge, and she made us make volcanoes **AGAIN.** How many times do we have to mix baking soda and vinegar? When do we get to use REAL chemicals? Dad says that when he was a kid, you could get all kinds of cool stuff you can't buy anymore. He even made his own fireworks. Except he blew up the driveway making them. I guess that's why you can't buy those ingredients now.

Omar was my volcano partner. We always try to be partners, since we're best friends.

OMAR ALWAYS WEARS A CAP. I USED TO THINK HE WAS BALD. NOW I KNOW HE'S JUST A CAP FREAK—HE HAS 63 DIFFERENT ONES!

VINEGAR

ME, WITH VOLCANO INGREDIENTS

BAKING SODA

Experiment #2
How to make a model volcano

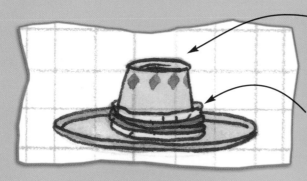

UPSIDE-DOWN PAPER CUP WITH BOTTOM CUT OFF

WAX PAPER, RUBBER-BANDED TO SEAL THE TOP OF THE CUP

Steps:

1. Add vinegar.
2. Add baking soda.
3. Watch it erupt.

(Add red food coloring to vinegar for lava-like color.)

Observations:

When vinegar hits baking soda, a rapid reaction happens. Foaming mess rises up and gushes over the cup.

Results:

Ta-da! You have successfully made a model of a volcanic eruption—just

DON'T EAT IT!

I wanted to make more interesting things than the same old—same old volcano, so Omar and I made a group of eraser people trying to flee the burning lava flow. But Ms. Blodge didn't think it was funny—or educational.

ERASERS ARE NOT PART OF THIS EXPERIMENT, BOYS. PUT THEM AWAY NOW . . . OR I'LL CONFISCATE THEM!

The dreaded "C" word!

CONFISCATE!

Things Ms. Blodge has already confiscated:

 MY EXTRA-LARGE RUBBER-BAND BALL—
IT TOOK A WHOLE MONTH TO MAKE!

MY FLATTENED PENNY,
SMUSHED BY THE TRAIN.

 MY FOLDING COMB THAT LOOKS LIKE A
SWITCHBLADE WHEN IT'S FOLDED
BUT OPENS INTO AN INNOCENT COMB.

Actually, the erupting lava reminded me of Mom and Dad when they fight. Why do grown-ups fight, anyway? Aren't they supposed to behave better than kids? What kind of example are they setting?

WITHOUT VILLAGERS FLEEING DRAMATICALLY—
BORING!

ERUPTING
VOLCANO

We put away those erasers FAST—no way did I want to add them to Ms. Blodge's haul. I wanted to make a whole army of erasers. Omar wanted to make eraser aliens. So we made both.

Army Erasers

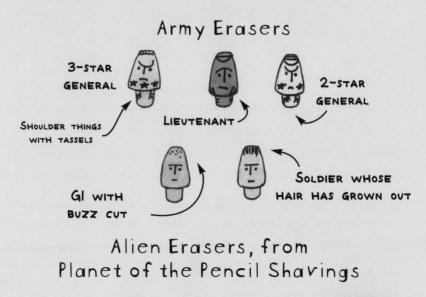

3-STAR GENERAL

SHOULDER THINGS WITH TASSELS

LIEUTENANT

2-STAR GENERAL

GI WITH BUZZ CUT

SOLDIER WHOSE HAIR HAS GROWN OUT

Alien Erasers, from Planet of the Pencil Shavings

WHICH ARE EYES, AND WHICH ARE NOSE HOLES? WITH ALIENS, WHO CAN TELL?

OMAR, WITH ALIENS EXPLORING THE BLACK HOLES OF NASAL SPACE.

Omar wanted us to make a comic book about the alien erasers. Here it is:

ALIEN ERASER

AND THE VOICE OF DOOM

GREETINGS, EARTHLING. I HAVE COME IN PEACE. TAKE ME TO YOUR LEADER.

IS THAT A REAL ALIEN?

HOW **DARE** YOU QUESTION MY REALNESS!

PREPARE TO HEAR **THE VOICE OF DOOM!**

NOT THAT! I BEG YOU!

I'LL TAKE YOU TO MY LEADER. JUST DON'T USE **THE VOICE OF DOOM.**

AND SO ALIEN ERASER IS TAKEN TO . . .

MS. KUTZ, MEET ALIEN ERASER.

HUH?

IS THIS ANOTHER ONE OF YOUR PRANKS? WELL, I'M IN NO MOOD FOR JOKES. YOU KNOW WHAT THIS MEANS, DON'T YOU?

UH-OH.

THE REAL VOICE OF DOOM:

CONFISCATION!

WHERE AM I?

POOR ALIEN ERASER IS SHUT IN A DRAWER WITH SQUIRT GUNS, BUBBLE GUM, AND OTHER LOOT MS. KUTZ HAS TAKEN AWAY FROM HER STUDENTS. WILL ALIEN ERASER EVER SEE THE LIGHT OF DAY AGAIN? FIND OUT IN THE NEXT ISSUE OF ALIEN ERASER!

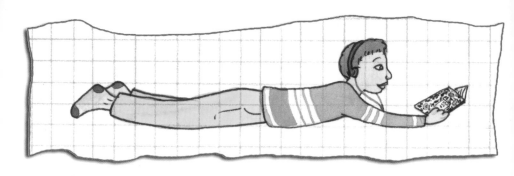

As boring as school is, some days it's a LOT better than home. Kevin stays in his room with his headphones surgically attached to his ears, so he can block things out. But I can't. I can't help but hear Mom and Dad yelling. Last night there was lots of door slamming, too. This morning Dad had already gone to work when I got up, but I could see from Mom's swollen, red eyes that she'd been crying.

I tried to cheer her up. "Great news, Mom! I'm working on an invention that turns sad, red eyes into clear, happy eyes," I said. Mom said she'd need much more than eye ointment to cure her problem.

DO YOU EVER LISTEN TO WHAT I SAY?

WHY SHOULD I? IT'S ALWAYS THE SAME OLD THING.

ERASER MOM   ERASER DAD

The walk to school was longer than ever.
My backpack felt like it was full of wet cement.
Omar could tell something was wrong.

WHAT'S UP WITH YOU, ANYWAY? YOU'RE NOT PLAYING WITH YOUR ERASER ARMY UNDER YOUR DESK.

I JUST DON'T FEEL LIKE IT.

YOU'RE NOT GONNA PUKE, ARE YOU?

DON'T WORRY— I WON'T PUKE.

Maybe Kevin knows what's going on with Mom and Dad—I'll ask him tonight. Only I'd better be prepared. Talking to Kevin can be like a very complicated experiment. You're hoping for a certain result, and in order to get it, special steps must be taken. Mom says Kevin is touchy because of hormones. Those are the same things that give him pimples. I think getting ugly bumps all over your face is reason enough to be grouchy!

Experiment #3
How to get a moody, easily irritated older brother in the mood to talk to his beloved younger brother

Ingredients:

One mug of hot chocolate
One plate of cookies
Two respectful raps on the door

Steps:

knock knock

1. When door opens a crack, quickly offer the hot chocolate and cookies. Brother should then allow access to his usually forbidden room.

2. Walk in. Put down mug and plate (NOT near the computer, or speedy ejection from room will follow).

3. Ask brother in a soft voice (very important— don't be loud or whiny) if you can talk to him for a minute.

Results:

It worked! Kevin actually let me in his room for five minutes.

But he didn't tell me much, not what I really wanted to know.

How should I know why Mom and Dad fight so much? Maybe they don't like each other anymore.

How can they not like each other? They're married.

Maybe they don't want to be married.

That was definitely **NOT** what I wanted to hear. Omar's parents are divorced, so I guess I could ask him what the warning signs are. I need to invent a Prevent-a-Divorce machine.

Invention #2: Happy-Marriages-R-Us Robots

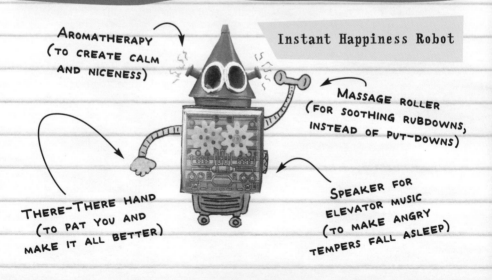

Instant Happiness Robot

Aromatherapy (to create calm and niceness)

Massage roller (for soothing rubdowns, instead of put-downs)

There-there hand (to pat you and make it all better)

Speaker for elevator music (to make angry tempers fall asleep)

Referee Robot

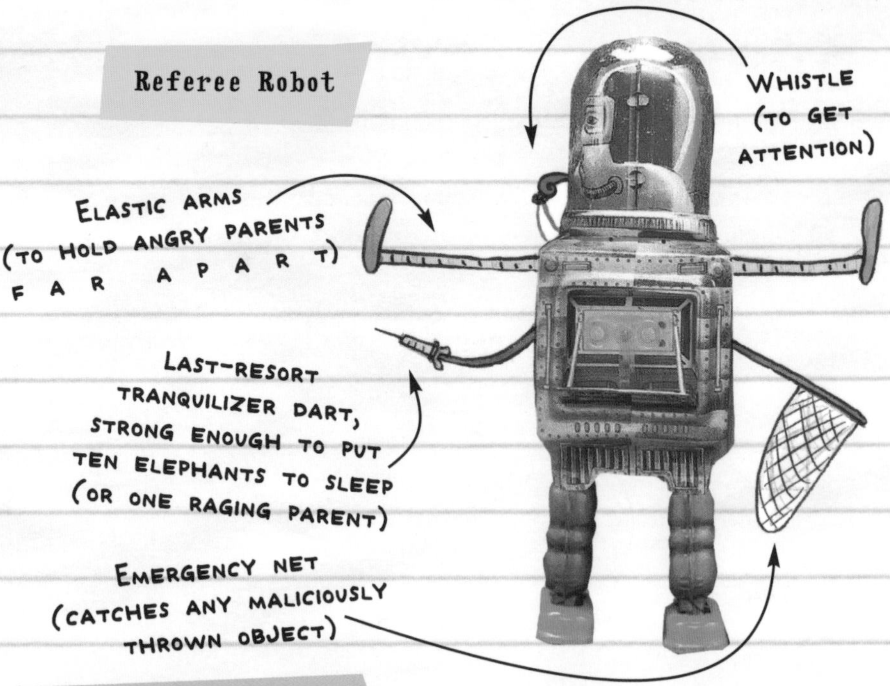

Whistle (to get attention)
Elastic arms (to hold angry parents f a r a p a r t)
Last-resort tranquilizer dart, strong enough to put ten elephants to sleep (or one raging parent)
Emergency net (catches any maliciously thrown object)

Soothe-a-Rama Robot

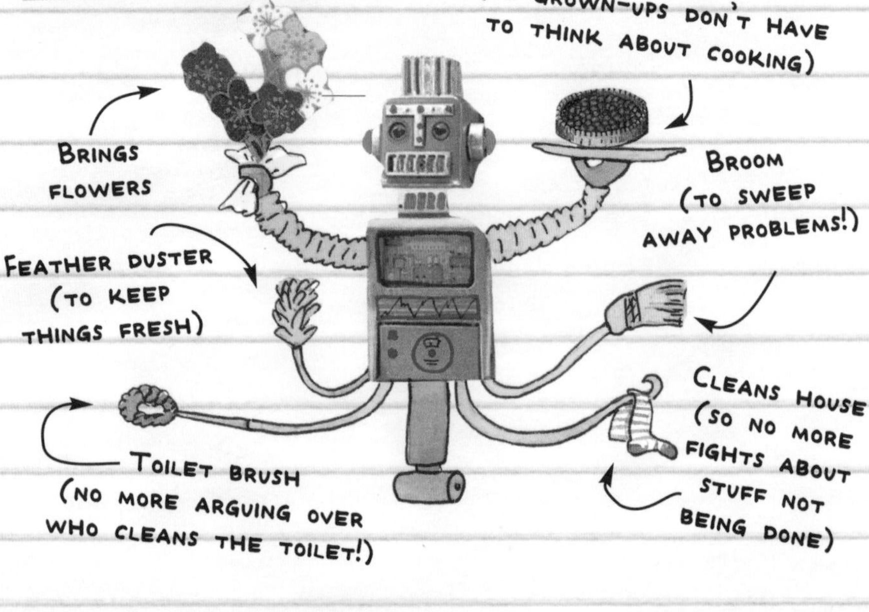

Makes meals (so grown-ups don't have to think about cooking)
Brings flowers
Broom (to sweep away problems!)
Feather duster (to keep things fresh)
Cleans house (so no more fights about stuff not being done)
Toilet brush (no more arguing over who cleans the toilet!)

Maybe I'm worried for nothing. Today, Dad promised to take me to his lab tomorrow and show me what he's working on. He hasn't done that in a long time! Since Dad was in a good mood, I wanted him to stay that way. I thought having his favorite dinner would help.

HEY, MOM, HOW ABOUT MEAT LOAF FOR DINNER? DAD LOVES THAT!

STEAM COMING OUT OF EARS

Mom made spaghetti instead. I know if we'd had meat loaf, things would have been different. Dad wouldn't have broken his promise. I know it.

I'M SORRY, MAX, BUT SOMETHING'S COME UP. YOUR MOTHER AND I REALLY NEED TO TALK. WE'LL GO TO THE LAB ANOTHER DAY, I PROMISE.

It's a bad sign when a parent says "your mother" or "your father" instead of "Mom" or "Dad." What I really need is something to make people keep their promises.

Invention #3
Hypnodisks

Stare into the whirling disks!

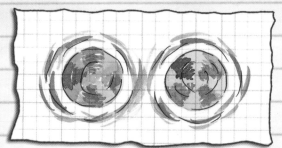

STARE,
STARE,
STARE!

You will do as I say.

MAKE MEAT LOAF!

TAKE ME TO YOUR LAB!

MEAT LOAF GOOD! MEAT LOAF YUM-YUM!

ZOMBIE MOM

ZOMBIE DAD

LAB GOOD! LAB FUN! COME TO GOOD, FUN LAB!

Too bad this wouldn't really work. I can make army and alien erasers do whatever I want, but not my parents.

New erasers to show Omar tomorrow:

GENERAL WITH ORDERS

SPECIAL-FORCES GUY WITH NIGHT-VISION BINOCULARS

SPECIAL-FORCES GUY WITH GPS SYSTEM

SPECIAL-FORCES GUY WITH K RATIONS

Omar thought my new erasers were really cool, so he made some alien blobs like them.

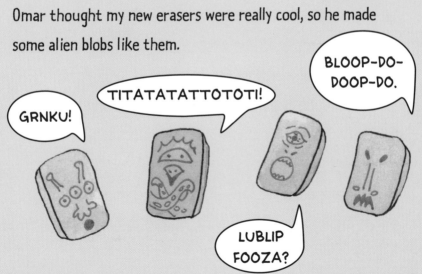

While he was working on them, I thought it was a good time to ask him about the whole divorce thing.

NICE BLOB, OMAR. DO YOU KEEP YOUR STUFF AT YOUR MOM'S OR YOUR DAD'S HOUSE? DOES IT FEEL WEIRD TO HAVE TWO HOUSES?

I KEEP STUFF AT BOTH PLACES, BUT MOSTLY AT MY MOM'S. IT'S NOT WEIRD ANYMORE, JUST ANNOYING SOMETIMES— ESPECIALLY WHEN I WANT SOMETHING THAT'S AT THE OTHER HOUSE.

I took a deep breath and said, "So you don't mind your parents being divorced?"

He didn't say anything for a while.

"Weeelll," he finally said, "it'd be better if they were still married . . . but not if they would fight the way they used to. Man, it got ugly!"

Divorce was better than fighting? I'm not so sure. I'd rather make comics with Omar than talk about divorce, anyway.

ALIEN ERASER IN How THE WIND BLOWS!

Now what, indeed? Is our hero destined for the dump or can he escape yet again? Find out in the next issue of ALIEN ERASER!

Ms. Blodge almost caught us drawing Alien Eraser's latest adventure. I definitely don't want her to confiscate that! (Besides, if she sees the word "fart," she'll give us detention for sure. She's like that.)

Evil-teacher erasers:

DETENTION!

CONFISCATION!

NOT TO MENTION!

PAY ATTENTION!

PAY ATTENTION, CLASS! TODAY WE HAVE A SPECIAL GUEST. MR. CABRILLO IS GOING TO TALK TO US ABOUT CONFLICT RESOLUTION.

THAT'S SETTLING OUR DIFFERENCES PEACEFULLY AND AVOIDING FIGHTS.

This could be just what I need! If I can get my parents to do this conflict-resolution stuff, maybe they won't get divorced!

MR. CABRILLO SMILED A LOT, LIKE IT'S SO MUCH FUN NOT TO FIGHT.

He had some kids act out situations that could have started fights but didn't, like accidentally elbowing somebody or stepping on someone's lunch by mistake. I'm not sure how useful his tips are. These aren't the kinds of things Mom and Dad fight about.

Then he had us write a list of facts about ourselves—things (not people) we like and don't like.

STUFF I LIKE / STUFF I DON'T LIKE

1. I LIKE INVENTING STUFF!
2. I LIKE DRAWING!
3. I LIKE BEING IN CONTROL!
4. I LIKE MAKING SOLDIERS AND ALIENS OUT OF ERASERS!
5. I LIKE BEING A BORN LEADER!
6. I LIKE MAKING COMICS WITH OMAR!
7. I LIKE WRITING EXCLAMATION POINTS!!!!!!!!
8. I DON'T LIKE HEARING MY PARENTS FIGHT!
9. I DON'T LIKE BROKEN PROMISES!
10. I DON'T LIKE LISTENING TO BORING LECTURES!
11. I DON'T LIKE BEING SENT TO DETENTION!
12. I DON'T LIKE HAVING MY STUFF CONFISCATED!
13. I DON'T LIKE ACTING IN STUPID SKITS!
14. I DON'T LIKE WRITING LISTS!

I LIKE ALL KINDS OF ROBOTS.

REMEMBER, NO PERSONAL REMARKS ABOUT OTHER PEOPLE.

BY THAT HE MEANT DON'T SAY, "I DON'T LIKE HOW MARTY ALWAYS PICKS HIS NOSE."

I LIKE how Marty does that!

I have no idea how making a list is supposed to keep us from fighting, but at least Mr. Cabrillo used up so much time that we missed math for the day.

I've decided to make some inventions that will show Mom and Dad how to get along.

Invention #4
Glitter Jar

1. IN A JAR, MIX RUBBING ALCOHOL WITH COOKING OIL.

2. ADD BEADS, SEQUINS, GLITTER, OR OTHER TINY SHINY THINGS.

3. ADD A LITTLE FOOD COLORING IF YOU WANT. SHAKE THE JAR.

THE OIL AND ALCOHOL DON'T MIX—THEY FIGHT— BUT TOGETHER THEY'RE VERY PRETTY.

Invention #5
Swirl-ee Bottle

IF YOU WANT "PRETTY," A SWIRL-EE BOTTLE IS GOOD.

1. FILL A BOTTLE ABOUT 1/4 FULL OF DISH SOAP
   (THE KIND WITH GLYCOL STEARATE IN IT).

2. ADD A COUPLE DROPS OF FOOD COLORING.

3. TRICKLE COLD WATER IN TO FILL UP BOTTLE.

4. CAP IT AND SWIRL!

WARNING! DON'T PUT THE WATER IN TOO QUICKLY OR YOU'LL HAVE A BOTTLE OF FOAM!

I gave Mom and Dad the glitter jar last night. I told them it was a scientific example of how two things (oil and alcohol) can fight but still work together to make something really cool. Since they're both scientists, I thought they'd get what I was saying. But they just looked at each other in a very sad way. I guess that invention's a dud.

To make up for not liking my glitter jar (he said he liked it, but he sure didn't look happy about it), Dad showed me an experiment. It was fun, but it was a sad kind of fun because neither one of us was happy.

Experiment #4
How do hot water and cold water react to each other?

Will the colors mix together and blend into purple, or stay separate and fight each other?

Steps:

1) FILL JAR #1 WITH HOT WATER. ADD RED FOOD COLORING.

2) FILL JAR #2 WITH COLD WATER. ADD BLUE FOOD COLORING.

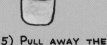

3) SEAL THE TOP OF THE RED JAR WITH AN INDEX CARD.

4) QUICKLY FLIP OVER THE RED JAR ON TOP OF THE BLUE JAR.

5) PULL AWAY THE INDEX CARD CAREFULLY. (HOLD ON TO THE JARS!)

Results:
Bad news! The colors don't want to mix! They fight! I said it was a sad experiment to have the colors stay separate like that. Dad smiled and said we should try it the other way around, with the blue jar on top. So we did.

AND THEY MIXED!

BEAUTIFUL,
BEAUTIFUL
PURPLE!

So maybe there's hope. Even though they might fight
sometimes, they can also blend together.

I didn't tell Mom and Dad about Mr. Cabrillo and conflict
resolution, but I told Kevin. He said Mr. Cabrillo had talked to
his class when he was my age, too.

When Mom kissed me good night, she told me not to worry.
I was afraid to ask what it is I'm not supposed to worry about.
Instead I just lay there in the dark—worrying.

Why do things always seem worse in the middle of the night?
Stomachaches hurt twice as much, noises are ten times scarier,
and small worries get bigger and bigger instead of going away.
And why do we worry, anyway? It's not useful—things don't get
better from worrying about them. You'd think we'd lose
worrying as we evolved, like we lost having a tail.

IF DAD CAN STOP LOVING MOM, CAN HE STOP LOVING ME?

WHO WOULD I LIVE WITH IF MOM AND DAD GOT DIVORCED?

WHO WOULD KEVIN LIVE WITH?

DARK CLOUDS OF WORRY

WOULD KEVIN DIVORCE ME, TOO?

WOULD MOM OR DAD REMARRY?

WOULD I HAVE EVIL STEPBROTHERS AND STEPSISTERS?

Now I know I have something to worry about. Mom and Dad called a family meeting for tonight after dinner.

I tried to eat, but the meatballs felt like lead balls, the applesauce was like cement, and the rice tasted like gritty sand.

It wasn't a meal; it was construction material.

The air in the room felt like a rubber band that had been

S T R E T C H E D

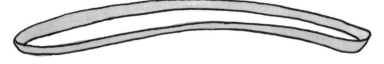

and was about to snap.

Poor rubber band!

And then the snap came—Mom said we must have noticed some tension between her and Dad, and they had decided it would be better for them to separate. Dad said he'd already found an apartment and would move out this weekend.

"We're still a family," Dad said. "I'll always be your dad." We're supposed to stay with Mom during the week, and every other weekend we'll stay with Dad. That's not my idea of a family.

THEN WE HAD A STIFF "FAMILY" HUG.

MOM LOOKED AT THE FLOOR.

ME, I DIDN'T KNOW WHERE TO LOOK OR WHAT TO FEEL.

KEVIN STARED STRAIGHT AHEAD, HIS FACE A BLANK.

DAD LOOKED MISERABLE.

IT WAS THE WORST NIGHT OF MY LIFE.

Dad said good-bye, and he was gone. You would think someone leaving your family would leave a big hole in the middle of the house, but Dad only took his stuff—little things—and left everything else the same.

NO MORE CRACKED COFFEE CUP THAT NO ONE DARED WASH BECAUSE DAD LIKES THE TASTE OF OLD GRIMY COFFEE MIXED WITH FRESH COFFEE.

NO MORE WEIGHTS IN THE LIVING ROOM TO PLAY WITH WHILE WATCHING MOVIES.

NO MORE EXTRA-LARGE RUBBER BOOTS TO STOMP AROUND IN, PRETENDING TO BE GODZILLA.

LET ME EAT TOKYO NOW!

This morning everything seemed weirdly normal, except Dad wasn't there (but he often leaves for work really early). It was like being in a "What's wrong with this picture?" puzzle, where at first you can't tell that anything is wrong. But if you look more closely . . .

Am I the ONLY one who notices someone is missing?

I wanted to tell Omar what was wrong, but I couldn't. Maybe if nobody knows my dad has moved out, it hasn't really happened. Maybe I imagined the whole thing.

Omar lined up his alien erasers, and I tried to play with him, but he could tell I wasn't really paying attention.

Then class started, and things got worse. Ms. Blodge was mad that I hadn't turned in my homework (yeah, yeah, I forgot it). I had to stay inside during recess to finish it. So I stayed inside. But I didn't do my homework. I worked on the comic instead.

ALIEN ERASER
IN
TRAPPED AGAIN!

Deep at the bottom of a trash can, Alien Eraser ponders his fate.

Here I am, sitting in—ew, GARBAGE!

I GOTTA GET OUTTA HERE!

BUT HOW?

Alien Eraser carefully examines the surrounding detritus, hoping to find something to use to escape.

This whoopee cushion already failed me once—and the rest of this stuff is . . .

. . . well, GARBAGE.

There's only one other way.

Depending entirely on his own superior rubberiness, Alien Eraser bounces himself against the bottom of the can, harder and harder until . . .

I'M FREE!

Yes! Our hero is safe once again . . . or is he? To find out, read the next issue of ALIEN ERASER!

Mom got hot chocolate and doughnuts
for Kevin and me after school.
She's never done that before. Then
Dad came to take me and Kevin out
for pizza. We ate and told bad jokes,
and things felt almost normal. Almost.
Until Dad dropped us back at the house
   as if he'd just been giving us a ride
   and wasn't part of our family.

SWEET
DOUGHNUT—TOO
SWEET AND
DOUGHY TODAY.

There was no pretending normal
then. Dad hugged Kevin and me,
and I could see he was crying.
So I whispered in his ear,
"Don't worry, Dad—
we'll invent another
kind of family."
And we will.
I know we will.

PEPPERONI PIZZA—
USUALLY MY
FAVORITE, BUT IT
DIDN'T TASTE RIGHT
SOMEHOW.

Looks tasty
to me.

I'm just not sure what kind of family we'll be. A family with a part-time dad? A half of a family? A family and a half?

If you take apart a family, can you put it back together in a way that makes sense?

When I figure out what kind of family we are now, then I guess I can draw a new picture of it.

I guess I'm kind of getting used to Dad being gone. We still haven't even seen his apartment, but Dad says that as soon as he gets things fixed up, he'll have Kevin and me over.

I wonder what his new home looks like—a pile of unpacked boxes, I bet.

DAD STUFF   MORE DAD   YET MORE
                 STUFF   DAD STUFF

Key to Dad's planet (or apartment)

Bloop! Bloop! Alien lava pits in Dad's kitchen

Extraterrestrial single-sock area— a dark, mysterious place where Dad claims all his socks run away to.

Burnt toast crusts— proof that Dad was here.

Intergalactic fetid stink pile of gross stuff Dad swears is good for houseplants (but what about those of us who have noses and are forced to smell it?).

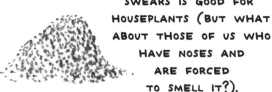

Mountain of shaving stubble— evidence of other life-forms existing in the universe.

Toilet paper roll desert wasteland— sign of an alien abduction?

Dad's place wasn't at all what I'd imagined. It was small and mostly empty, like a doctor's waiting room. We played cards and ate popcorn, but even that didn't make it feel cozier.

After Dad went to bed, Kevin and I stayed up talking.

I KNOW DAD'S STILL DAD, BUT THIS FEELS DIFFERENT.

GOOD DIFFERENT OR BAD DIFFERENT?

I'M NOT SURE. MAYBE BOTH.

WELL, MAYBE IT'S YOU WHO'S DIFFERENT. NOW LET'S GO TO SLEEP.

Then I had the weirdest dream.

Nighty-night!

All my alien erasers were alive, and they were showing me
their planets. It was a galactic tour, kind of. Each place was
cool in a different way.

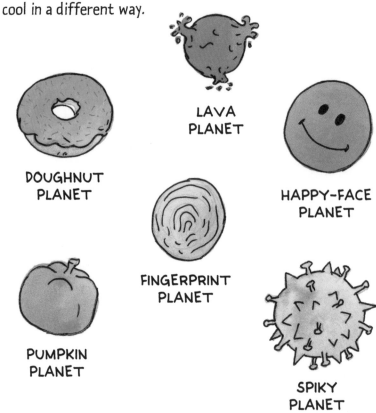

LAVA
PLANET

DOUGHNUT
PLANET

HAPPY-FACE
PLANET

FINGERPRINT
PLANET

PUMPKIN
PLANET

SPIKY
PLANET

Then I came to a planet that was perfect for me, full of
inventions and experiment stuff. And I knew that that
was where I belonged.

But in front of me were two doors. Did I have to choose between them? I wasn't sure which door to go through.

One door led to my bedroom at home.

The other door opened into Dad's new apartment.

Then a voice suddenly boomed:

Greetings from Alien Eraser!
Welcome to Max's world!
Yes, this is YOUR planet. You can go
through any door that you want,
whenever you want.

"I don't have to choose one or the other?" I asked.

"You put your right foot in;
you put your right foot out.
You put your left foot in, and
you shake it all about.
You step into the left
room, you step into the
right, you put your both
feet in, and

you're feeling outta sight!"

Luckily I woke up before I had to do the hokeypokey. The funny thing was, even though Dad's apartment was still a strange place, now it definitely didn't look or feel like an alien world. And Kevin's snoring sounded just like home.

What was really weird, though, was that I found an Alien Eraser inside my sleeping bag. How did that get there? Is this a message from another planet?

wink
wink

Copyright © 2003, 2009 by Marissa Moss

First paperback edition 2009

Library of Congress Cataloging-in-Publication Data is available.
Library of Congress Catalog Card Number 2008937046

ISBN 978-0-7636-3577-0 (hardcover)
ISBN 978-0-7636-4407-9 (paperback)

4 6 8 10 9 7 5 3

Printed in China

This book was typeset in Kosmic Plain One, with hand-lettered type by the author-illustrator.
The illustrations were done in colored pencil, gouache, watercolor, ink, and collage.

Candlewick Press
99 Dover Street
Somerville, Massachusetts 02144

visit us at www.candlewick.com

To Elias,

the inspiration for it all,

and to the memory of Harvey, his wonderful father,

who will live within us always

Alien Eraser
in
To the Rescue

Alien Eraser slides the logbook under the boy's pillow.

The next morning . . .

The book is discovered.

And so the story of Alien Eraser begins in a boy's bedroom somewhere in Ordinaryville, deep in the heart of Plainplace, USA.

But it travels far beyond the confines of that place to the broadest reaches of the universe.

Up, up, and away!

My work has just begun! I sense there is a problem with the earth boy. I must help him.

With my superior brain, I'm sure I can find a solution for his woes.

I just have to look far enough and think hard enough.

Aha! The answer is coming to me — something to do with the hokeypokey!

Will Alien Eraser find a way to rescue the boy, or will he have to dance the hokeypokey by himself? To find out, look for the next episode of ALIEN ERASER!

Marissa Moss is the author–illustrator of the extremely popular Amelia's Notebook series, which now numbers twenty-eight titles. In addition, she has written and illustrated more than a dozen picture books, some historical fiction, and an ancient Egyptian mystery for older readers. The idea of writing stories in a notebook style came to her when she was buying school supplies for her son. She spotted a black-and-white composition book that reminded her of a notebook she had had when she was a kid. "So I bought it—for myself, not my son," she says, "and I wrote and drew what I remembered from when I was his age." She started drawing comics in high school, first in her notebook, then as a comic strip for the school paper, but the Max Disaster books have given her a chance to combine her love of inventions, experiments, and comics all in one place. Marissa Moss was born in Pennsylvania but moved to California when she was two and has lived there ever since. She studied art at San José State, history at the University of California at Berkeley, and art again at the California College of the Arts. Marissa Moss lives in the San Francisco Bay Area with her family.